Peppa Pig™

George's First Day at Playgroup

Today is George's first day at playgroup.

"Isn't George too small for playgroup?" asks Peppa.

"You can look after him," says Daddy Pig.

Peppa isn't sure she wants George at her playgroup, but she likes the idea of looking after him.

"Are you sure George is big enough?"

Peppa asks when they arrive.

"Yes, he'll be fine," replies Daddy Pig.

"OK. He can come," says Peppa.

She holds onto George's hand.

"Grunt! Grunt!" snorts George, jumping

up and down.

Here is Madame Gazelle, Peppa's playgroup teacher. She looks after Peppa and her friends. Madame Gazelle tells the children that George is coming to play. The children are all very excited about meeting Peppa's little brother.

George shakes his toy, Mr Dinosaur, at Madame Gazelle, "Grrr! Dine-saw!"

"Aah! Really scary!" laughs Madame Gazelle. Peppa is proud of George making everyone laugh. "George is my little brother. He's brilliant," she says.

"George is not very good at painting," says Peppa. "But I can show him how to paint a flower."

"Watch me, George," snorts Peppa.
"First, you paint a big circle."

Peppa carefully dips her brush into a pot of
pink paint and draws a big pink circle
right in the middle of her paper.

George draws a big green circle.

"No, George. That's the wrong colour,"

snorts Peppa. "Watch me."

Peppa makes yellow petal shapes.

George paints a green zigzag.

"George! That's the wrong shape," says Peppa.

Peppa admires her flower painting.
"Perfect," she says, happily.
George is still painting. Instead of a stalk
and leaves he has painted another circle
with five lines sticking out from it.
"You are doing it all wrong!" says Peppa.

"I've painted a flower," says Peppa.
"Very good, Peppa," smiles Madame Gazelle.
"And look, George has painted a dinosaur."
Madame Gazelle sticks Peppa and George's
pictures on the wall.